Ladybird  Readers

In the Mud

Notes to teachers, parents, and carers

The *Ladybird Readers* Starter Level gently introduces children to the phonics approach to reading, by covering familiar themes that young readers will have studied (for example, colors, animals, and family).

Phonics focuses on how the individual sounds of letters are blended together to sound out a word. For example, **/c/ /a/ /t/** when put together sound out the word **cat**.

The Starter Level is divided into two sub-level sections:
- **A** looks at simple words, such as **ant**, **dog**, and **red**.
- **B** explores trickier sound–letter combinations, such as the **/igh/** sound in **night** and **fright**.

This book looks at the theme of **friends** and focuses on these sounds and letters:
m oi ue or ear

There are some activities to do in this book. They will help children practice these skills:

 Spelling and writing   Speaking   Reading

LADYBIRD BOOKS

UK | USA | Canada | Ireland | Australia
India | New Zealand | South Africa

Ladybird Books is part of the Penguin Random House group of companies
whose addresses can be found at global.penguinrandomhouse.com.
www.penguin.co.uk   www.puffin.co.uk   www.ladybird.co.uk

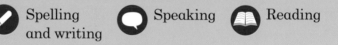 Penguin Random House UK

First published 2017
001

Printed in China
A CIP catalogue record for this book is available from the British Library

ISBN: 978–0–241–29913–5

All correspondence to:
Ladybird Books
Penguin Random House Children's
80 Strand, London WC2R 0RL

MIX
Paper from
responsible sources
FSC® C018179

Ladybird Readers

In the Mud

Look at the story

Series Editor: Sorrel Pitts
Story by Coleen Degnan-Veness
Illustrated by Ian Cunliffe

Picture words

Blue Boy

Orange Boy

Green Boy

Purple Boy

Aa Bb Cc Dd Ee Ff Gg Hh Ii Jj Kk Ll Mn

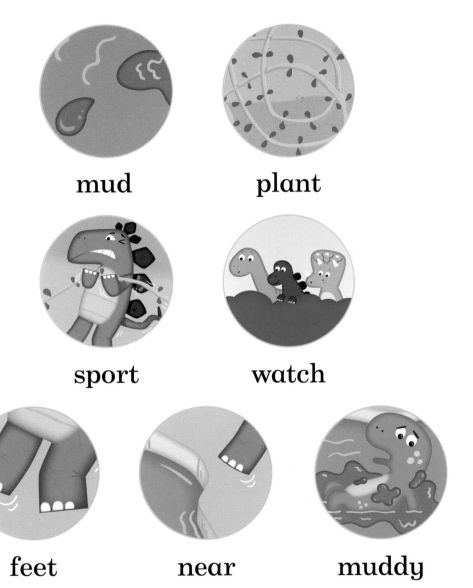

mud

plant

sport

watch

feet

near

muddy

Use these words to help you with the activity on page 16.

Blue Boy   **Purple Boy**

mud muddy

7

Purple Boy

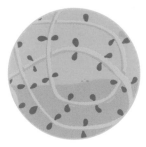

plant

sport

Orange Boy   **Green Boy**

watch

feet   **near**

13

muddy

15

Activity

1 Look. Say the sounds.
Write the letters. 📖 🗨 ✏

| or | oy | ue |

1 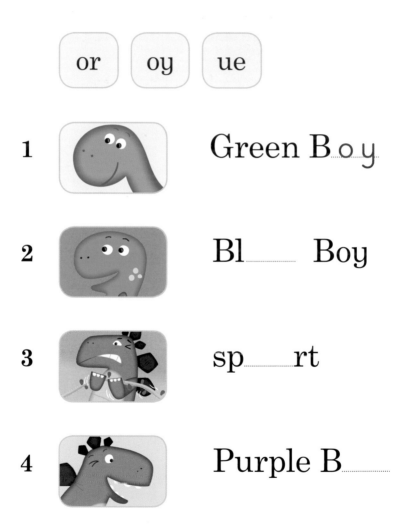 Green B o y

2 Bl____ Boy

3 sp____rt

4 Purple B____

16

In the Mud

Read the story

Purple Boy is bad. He puts Blue Boy in the mud.

Blue Boy is muddy now!

19

Blue Boy thinks. He gives a long plant to Purple Boy.

21

Orange Boy speaks to Green Boy.

Blue Boy wants Purple Boy in the mud. Let's watch!

22

Blue Boy puts
the plant here.

This is my
favorite
sport!

24

Purple Boy's feet are near the mud.

Purple Boy is muddy now!

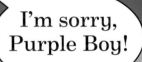

I'm sorry, Purple Boy!

I'm sorry, Blue Boy!

Activities

2 **Look and read. Match.**

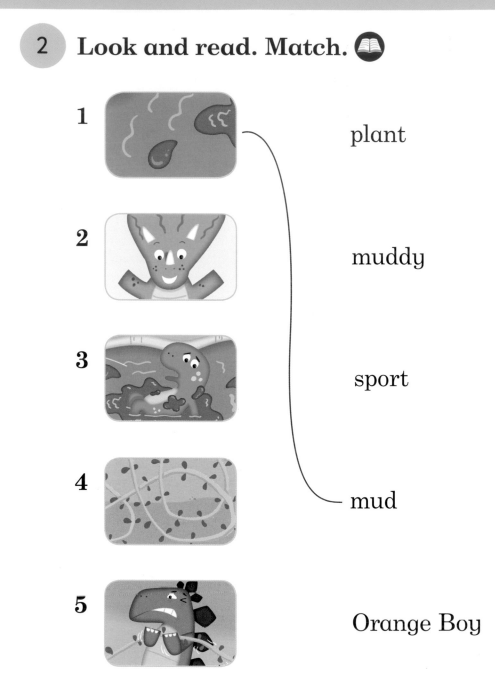

1   plant

2   muddy

3   sport

4   mud

5   Orange Boy

3 Look. Say the sounds.
Write the letters.

or   m

1 I'm ___ m uddy!

2 I know a good sp___t!

3 This is ___y
favorite sp___t!

4 Find the words.

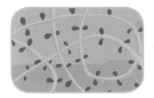
plant

watch

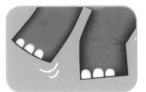
feet

near

muddy

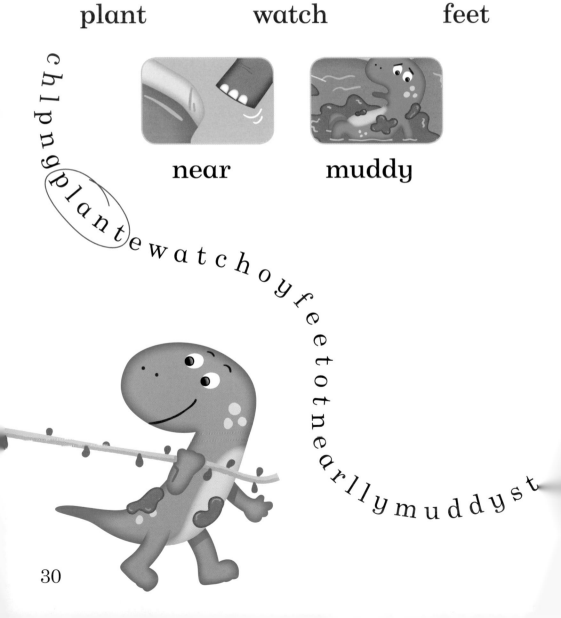

chlpngplantewatchoyfeetotnearllymuddyst

30

5 Read the words. Draw the pictures and color them in.

Blue Boy has got a long plant.

Purple Boy is in the mud!

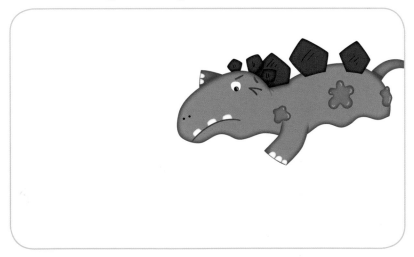

Starter Level A and B

The Zoo
978-0-241-28346-2

Dom Dog and his Boat
978-0-241-28340-0

Ted in Bed
978-0-241-28342-4

The Fun Run
978-0-241-28343-1

Nicky and Poppy
978-0-241-29912-8

Doctor Panda
978-0-241-28339-4

Farmer Carl
978-0-241-28341-7

The Old Boat
978-0-241-28345-5

Brother Blue
978-0-241-20338-7

In the Mud
978-0-241 29913-5

The Big Fish
978-0-241-29915-9

Gus is Hot!
978-0-241-29914-2